Presence

TALES OF CHARLES ISLAND
TALE 1

Marissa D'Angelo

Cover design by Amanda Grillo

This story is fiction. Although the place exists, the characters, plot and dialogues in this book are fictional. Resemblance to any persons living or dead is coincidental.

Printed in the United States of America

Dedication

To my father:

Thank you for never leaving my side,
even through death I refuse to believe you are
truly gone

Author's Note

Since the release of this book, I have wanted to find some way to help Charles Island and the wildlife that it supports. A local reforestation group is working hand in hand with the Connecticut Department of Energy and Environmental Protection to plant more trees so that the island and its wildlife can survive and thrive.

Message from Reforestation Group:

We want to restore the island to its former state. After years of invasive species and diseases, we need to help nature along with this task.

10% of the proceeds from this series will go to this cause.

Foreword

Something about this place always brought me back — whether it be a joyful mood that I wanted to share with others or the calm of the sea that drew me in. Looking out and wondering about the history of the island had always filled my mind with an endless curiosity. This past time, I had met a man who told me of the history that the island and shores held. His fascination soon became my own and thus the impenetrable admiration caused my imagination to flourish all the more.

A recent series of losses sparked my search for questions that could not be answered simply. Upon visiting day after day, I had run into a preacher who reminded me of life's infinite ways. Accepting the loss of my father was difficult to forego until I realized that I do not need to accept it because it is not true. The very existence of one's soul never truly leaves this universe – the form changes. What happens to the soul after it leaves the body? No one knows. One can just ponder that deep in thought.

Island

1

The calm of the waters always drew people in. A salty taste filled the air along with seagulls chattering about for their next meal. The murky blue pushed many different shells and sea creatures about. Tides brought them up to the sandy shores only to send them back out to sea. They judged where you could go. Sometimes, they would be as close as the nearby grass while other times, the sea would reveal its hidden features.

Many people came to enjoy the beach, but all that visited could not miss the sight of the island.

From the coastline, it seemed small, but the closer

you would get, the vaster it truly became. Travelers

and even nearby residents soon learned of the ways

of the island. If you visited by foot, you had to wait

until low tide. At that point, and only then, the rocky

causeway to the island appeared through the

depths of the water. Seagulls would hover above

this path as if they were the gatekeepers to the

island. You could walk there, but only during this

short time. As soon as the tide came in, the path

disappeared.

Several, if not many, visitors ventured out and

were unable to make it back to the coast in time

because the tide concealed their way back home.

They would still try anyway and were quickly met

with the harsh rip currents of the sea as it carried them out, unable to call for help or be heard.

However, trips that were planned accordingly went very smoothly as you could discover the beauty that this island did hold. After crossing the path, one would find many different creatures and plants. The most abundant were birds that seemed to circle it endlessly. Several birds including herons, egrets and piping plovers called this place their home. There was a thin strip of sandy shore that outlined the island's perimeter and a dense jungle lied within. From afar, the jungle looked bare with just a few trees. Once you got there, you could see the variety of trees, vines and other remains. But you could only view it from its exterior. The inside was

marked off by fencing that claimed bird habitats
resided within.

The island's original name was Poquahaug which
meant cleared land, named by the Paugussett tribe.
After the Europeans took this land from the Native
Americans, the Paugussett cursed it and any
buildings ever built upon its soil. All warnings were
ignored as a tobacco plantation was built on it in
1657 by Charles Deal, which is where the islands
present name comes from - Charles Island.

Despite the many signs of caution, there were
still quite a few people who disobeyed these words
as their curiosity drew them in anyway. One of whom
had been a young photographer that found himself

in a daze when it came to the island's hypnotizing

grasp.

Adam

2

The city streets felt crowded even when there weren't many people wandering about. Adam Moor hated the constant cars honking, smell of old hot dogs reheated to sell in huts for people desperate enough to eat their food and, of course, how people shoved into him as they passed as if he was invisible. Nevertheless, he still managed to be stuck here.

Today, he hurried to one of many interviews he had gone on to land a job in photography. Only problem was everyone and their phones now thought of themselves as professional photographers… They tended to get quite lucky with some of their shots and the new devices that came out definitely had good cameras. He used a professional camera that had been handed down to him from his father. Although he aspired to be just like him, the two couldn't have been more different, or so Adam thought.

His father was a tall man that stood out like a twig. Seemed to have no meat on his bones. A hint of scoliosis sent his back into the slightest of curves. He always kept a clean-shaven face and wore a cold-pressing stare with grey stone eyes while Adam had his mother's piercing green eyes. The angle of his nose protruded out like its own monument on his blank face.

Adam had caramel skin like his mother from Sicily. He hadn't heard much about her other than the fact that she had left when he was just a child. He had light brown, sandy hair and kept it cut short. There were many toddler pictures where his locks were down to his shoulders making him easily mistaken for a little girl. He always shuddered at the thought of finding those pictures and asking his mom if that was his sister. Never again.

Mr. Moor was extremely old fashioned when it came to certain routines and just living life. He was a great man, but most of the time was pensive and a workaholic. Most, if not all, conversations between him and his son revolved around school and politics growing up. And, of course, photography. His father raised him since he was very young to take all kinds of photos. Animals, people, landscapes, sunsets… They would even wake up before the crack of dawn to snap some sunrises.

Adam tried his best to hold interest in photography, as he actually became quite good at it. He longed to draw these sunsets and animals much more though.

After high school, Mr. Moor promised to pay for Adam's college, but on one condition: that he majored in photography. Adam had to agree to these great terms, but still managed to minor in art just to keep himself motivated throughout college, which seemed to be quite a blur as he immersed himself in his work and even more so in painting.

There were many times where he would prepare photos for his classes, but then fall into drawing the pictures that he had captured. So, he spent much of his time in college catching up on missed work.

He was just out of college when he received the news of his father's tragic passing. Unfortunately, Mr. Moor had been in quite a bit of debt, so most was taken that had been in his name. The belongings from within his home went to Adam, but he sadly remained with a college degree and great camera that he thought he had no use for. His art dreams were quickly pushed to the back of his mind while reality set in as he had to figure out how to make a living by himself. He decided to pursue photography as Mr. Moor would have wanted.

So, here he was at the umpteenth newspaper agency applying for some type of job…This one was a division of one of the still-surviving newspapers for the city. The post had been listed online:

HELP WANTED!

PHOTOGRAPHERS FOR…

TRAVEL COLUMN

NEEDED!

Adam remembered finding the job listing and being met with utter shock deep within his chest as he realized that the job was in fact his father's job before he had passed. For days and days, he set the listing aside because he couldn't stand the thought of setting foot back in his father's office. Instead of forgetting about it, he would come back to the listing and think it was some type of sign so he decided to contact them. When he made the call, the secretary was more than eager to book an appointment for an interview with him as soon as he said who he was.

So there he stood in front of his father's old agency. He looked up at the building, which seemed much smaller to him now that he was an adult. Back when he was little and visited with his dad, the building felt as though it towered over him.

He walked in and was instantly met with a strong wall of the cool air conditioning. He was dying in his dress shirt and slacks as it was. So this jolt felt nice and refreshing. There was a marbled-out lobby with 4 elevators, 2 on each side. Between each were directories. His eyes carefully scanned the list and found it:

Current Digest - Floor 3

He pressed in the button to go up and the flickering light behind illuminated it in a fiery orange glow. After a few seconds, the doors opened up and one person stood in the corner of the elevator. She just stared down at the floor not even acknowledging Adam. He got in and selected Floor 3. The top floor, 7, was also illuminated.

The silence overwhelmed him. Usually there would be elevator music of some sort, but all Adam could hear was the sound of waves crashing as if he was near the ocean. He glanced behind him at the quiet woman in the corner.

She had her brunette hair back in a braided bun as a professional worker would wear. She wore a dark gray dress that's length fell down to the floor, hiding her feet entirely. The top of the dress had buttons that went all the way up to her neck. She definitely looked as if she had come from another time. Suddenly, she lifted her head and locked her eyes on Adam's. Her pupils were colossal, rounded black holes that made Adam jerk his head back and stare at the front of the elevator again. His sweaty palms rested at his side while he kept his gaze on the ceiling of the elevator, monitoring her every move in the mirror. Something about her made him want to run and not look back.

After what seemed like several minutes of a slow-moving elevator, it stopped at the third floor. He got out and when he turned back to give a friendly wave goodbye, the lady was somehow no longer there in the corner.

He didn't get much sleep; his mind was probably just playing tricks on him. Adam shrugged it off and refocused his energy, still spooked. He looked down at his watch that read 11:15. He would be just above 10 minutes early to the interview.

The Interview

3

The newspaper's office was very well-kept and strangely uncrowded…Well, not so strange since most people get their news on the internet as opposed to newspaper nowadays. Adam was expecting something out of the movies where the office had several secretaries with phones ringing off the wall and people rushing in and out with news stories. Instead, there was just one lone secretary and the lobby was bare.

A dark blue carpet made up the lobby and there were several wooden tables with their edges and legs chipped. He could tell they were there for a long time. Maybe they were even older than him?

The walls were blank other than a single newspaper

in a frame with the headline:

PONSKY DOES IT AGAIN!

Of course they would be proud of political

coverage of the president...

A lady sat behind what looked like a secretary's

desk, so he assumed her title. She had just gotten

off the phone when she acknowledged him.

"Adam Moor?" She said, snapping Adam out of

his distractions. She stood up and made her way

over to him, reaching her hand out.

"Yes ma'am, you can call me Adam," he walked over to her and shook her delicate hand. "I'm a little early."

"It looked like something was troubling you, everything going okay?" she caught on fast. His mind raced back to the woman in the elevator.

"I just thought I saw someone in the elevator on the way here, but then she wasn't there any longer. It's probably nothing though," he said – immediately wishing he could take back the words he just said as he sounded like a loon.

"Hmm, that's strange. Everyone else in this building is away on vacation. It's just me and Mr. Dorpin. Maybe she just got lost, who knows… Your dad used to work here. We were very impatient for your visit! Go on back, last door on the left. The editor, Mr. Dorpin, should be ready for you!"

Oddly enough, he did not think they would be awaiting him so eagerly. But then again, he thought the place would be more crowded and look how that turned out.

She made him feel like a celebrity with her flashy smile and flushed cheeks. Her palm had been sweaty when he shook her hand. He didn't want to make her more nervous than she already appeared to be so he nodded his head and made his way back.

Just past the secretary's desk, there was a hallway that seemed longer than it was. With each step, the floorboards beneath the runner creaked.

They announced his arrival before he could introduce himself. As if he hadn't been heard, Adam politely knocked on the door to be met with a…

"Come on in, have a seat Adam!"

He made his way into Mr. Dorpin's office and was surprised to see that his dad's stories of Mr. Dorpin sure weren't exaggerated. He was a man of short stature. A baggy suit and tie seemed to suck his body in. He wore glasses that were drawn down to the edge of his wide nose. Adam could remember his dad's words that seemed to describe him to a T. They had been good friends since grade school. Mr. Moor being so immersed in his work, he never got to introduce them. Adam walked over to his desk and sat down across from him.

Mr. Dorpin jumped up and walked right over to where Adam sat. He comfortably rested each of his hands on Adam's shoulders.

"Wow, you surely take after your mother, huh?" He smiled and signaled Adam to follow him into the hallway. "There's something I want to show you."

Although Adam had just sat down as instructed, he got back up and followed suit to find out where they were headed. This was the strangest interview he had ever been on.

It took a short time as they were in front of the room adjacent to Mr. Dorpin's office. Mr Dorpin reached into his back pocket and pulled out a chain of keys. One with a green sticker dot stood out and he used it to unlock the door. Adam could hear the satisfying sound of the metallic key pressing against the lock until it clicked and unlocked the door that slowly opened.

"Um, Mr. Dorpin…what is in here that you are showing me?" Adam asked.

"Call me Jim. This is your father's office and I'd like to extend it to you now." He said as he patted Adam on the back. "Go on, check it out."

Adam looked over at Jim to see his reassuring smile as if he had just won the golden ticket. The room was overwhelmingly dark. He peered in and flicked on the light.

Mr. Moor's Office

4

A musty stench filled the air. This room had been abandoned and untouched for quite some time.

In the opposite corner from the door was a deep brown, mahogany desk with various papers scattered about the surface. The once bleached paper was now gray and covered in dust. The walls were covered in a 1970's striped wallpaper that met…what once was…a white trim in the middle. Below that was solid maroon paint, chipped and peeled in many places. The top portion of the wall was covered by framed articles and the like. Adam treaded lightly about the perimeter of the room, taking in each frame. After walking past several, he

stopped at one in particular that seemed to stand

out to him. He read the headlines of the newspaper

print:

PHOTOGRAPHER'S MYSTERY FIND

His father was in this photo next to the article

holding a frame of a woman that looked as if she

was from another era. Adam leaned closer and read

the article next to the photo.

Missing portrait found by photographer, Allen

Moor, on his travels to remote island just off the

east coast's shore.

The portrait is from the island's days of

hosting a resort for travelers all around the

world. It is said to be of "Lady Angeline," a wealthy woman whose father had left her the island after his sudden death. The hotel that she ran out of the center boomed and was all anyone could talk about in the mid-1800's. Unfortunately, rumors had spread that the hotel was non-functional and unsafe for its guests. Less and less people went to the island in wake of the rumors. Shortly after the Civil War, families stopped visiting the resort due to safety concerns and every building on the island met its fiery demise as they were suspiciously set on fire. Soon thereafter, there was no sign of Lady Angeline. She had vanished, it seemed, into thin air.

The abandoned hotel went up in flames. From vandals? Maybe. This island that had originally belonged to the natives was given back and they have protected the animals dwelling there to this day.

Mr. Moor's finding serves as living proof that Lady Angeline existed.

Adam took another look at the familiar face in the photo.

"Hey where did my dad end up putting this portrait? Did he sell it?" He asked Jim who still stood in the doorway. Jim didn't even have to come over to look at what portrait he was talking about.

"Oh, we put that one in the closet. Mina, the secretary, always hated looking at that when she had to come in to dust. It was a pretty interesting find of your father's. Not to mention one of the creepiest."

Adam headed over to the closet, curiosity peaked. Once he opened the door, he was surprised to find an empty little room with a frame faced in, concealing the front portrait. It was completely covered in a thick film of dust. He brought it out and wiped the dust away with his sleeve. As soon as the portrait was revealed, Adam felt his fingers go numb and the portrait fell from his hands to the ground. It fell to its side and the glass shattered all over the closet. Adam jumped back, apologetic.

"I'm so sorry! Do you have a broom? I can sweep this up." He said.

"No worries, Mina?! Get the dustpan and broom, please!" Jim yelled out into the hall. He rushed over to Adam and asked if he was alright while Adam just stood there pale and unable to find the words.

Mina entered the room in a hurry and eagerly cleaned up the mess.

"What on earth happened?!" She noticed the frame shattered. "Well, glad someone found a way to break this creepy thing!"

The portrait was intact, but the frame totaled for certain.

"Hey, let's walk back to my office and talk about your first assignment, is that good?" Jim put his hand on Adam's back and led him into the hall and back into his office. Adam felt himself sink down into the chair that he was sitting in before.

"Alright, get comfortable. You ok there? A little bit of a butter fingers back there, huh? I know it must have been difficult to go into your father's office. Maybe that was too soon on my part…" he said as he sat down on the other side of his desk and got out some papers.

It was not too soon, but Adam could have sworn that he saw that lady in the elevator. The one who had disappeared as he left. It would sound crazy to Jim so he kept it to himself, but knew he had to find out more about this.

The Assignment

5

Sometime while Jim was shuffling through papers,
Adam snapped out of his spooked state. He thought
about the upcoming assignment that he would have
to go on. It seemed to him that he had already
landed the job as this wasn't the typical interview. He
knew that Jim sent his father on the most random
assignments so he was eager to hear what was next
for him.

The first thing he did was bring out a map and
placed it right in front of Adam. Crouching over the
map, he brought his finger to the city that they lived
in.

"Here's where we are now…" then he dragged his finger over to the right of the map and said, "I'd like you to go here."

It was a small island off the New England coast. This was where his father had first gone when he tried catching photos of paranormal activity. Jim seemed to feel Adam's repulsion.

"Don't worry - just pictures of the bird habitat in the center of the island! We're doing a report on it. The environment folks want it."

It took Adam a few moments to process the request. Should he go against his gut and do it? If he didn't, he would spend his life wondering what could have been. But still, he kept replaying his dad's words in his head. "Whatever you do, go anyplace but there. It is a jail of wonder as soon as

you set foot on the island." But his father's words

only made him more interested in the very idea.

Besides, it was just pictures of birds anyway.

    "I'll take it. When do I start?"

Settling

6

Adam knew from his father that you couldn't drive to the island. Jim had booked a stay at a nearby bed and breakfast. Adam thought of it as a little vacation. He still couldn't push the memory of the woman in the elevator from his mind. He could have sworn she was actually there and looked just like the woman from the portrait in his father's office. He wished that he could share it with someone without sounding crazy but knew it would be best to just keep it to himself.

Prior to leaving his apartment in the city, he arranged for his neighbor to take care of his cat,

Milo. Milo was a gray tabby cat with black stripes and a white belly. He looked like he wore socks since he had white front and back legs. Milo was a pretty easy-going cat and Adam couldn't have asked for a better roommate other than the occasional trouble-maker things that he would do from time to time such as scratching the couch.

Adam walked out with his keys in one hand and a rolling luggage in the other. He practically had to squeeze himself out of the door because Milo came running as if he wanted to come.

"Not this time, buddy. Maybe next time. I won't be long and you'll be in good hands. I left Tom and Jerry on for you and some extra treats in your bowl." Although Milo continued towards the door, Adam reluctantly closed it or he would be late to check-in. He walked next door to his neighbor's apartment to give him the keys and gave a few knocks.

"Hey Adam," his neighbor, Steve, answered right away. His dirty blond hair was shagged over his face and uncombed. Under his eyes were dark circles probably from staying on the computer for far too long. He was in his pajamas still and it was around 3 o'clock in the afternoon. The wonders of working from home...

"Thanks again for watching Milo, I really appreciate it. I should be gone for just a week," he held out the keys.

"Of course, man. Have a safe trip!" Steve said as he took the keys and closed his door.

After a few hours of driving, Adam finally arrived. Unlike the city, these suburbs weren't lit as well and he almost passed right by the driveway to the small ranch. When he parked in the vacant lot, he used the flashlight on his phone to find the path to the front door and knocked.

"Be right there!" A lady's hoarse voice yelled over. Definitely a smoker. Adam set down his luggage and looked around. The bed and breakfast was a small, white ranch of a house. It looked quite old judging by the cracks in the shingles and squeaky front porch that left him weary he may fall through at any moment. The street was lit by several streetlamps, one going on and off constantly.

"Hey there, Adam! Long time no see!" The lady of short stature grabbed his smaller luggage and headed in. He couldn't quite figure out what she meant by that. He did faintly remember going with his dad on some assignments and maybe they had stayed there? Adam smiled nervously and followed the woman.

As soon as he stepped in the door, he immediately took in the 1970's vibe of the walls, furniture and pretty much everything else in the place. He made a side note that his father must have used the same decorator for his office as it looked incredibly similar. The floors were covered in a dark brown rug which matched the wood paneling along the walls. There were many figurines on shelves around the room. The main room which he had first entered in had a small desk in the corner and two large couches on the side adjacent to the desk. A small coffee table sat in front of the couches with several magazines scattered atop.

"I'm Wendy. Jim called us and we are so happy to have you. We gave your father residence many years back. You were very young but came with him too sometimes. It's been so long since we've seen you; you got so big! Please come this way to your room." Adam seemed to have a fuzzy memory when it came to this place, but he went along with it. The lady did look quite familiar after all.

Once again, Adam got that feeling of regret in his gut. He felt as though he was following in his father's exact footsteps. Still, he needed this job.

Wendy had a pale white face with bags under her eyes that made her look as if she hadn't slept in days…maybe weeks. She had her dirty blond/grey hair back in a ponytail and wore no make-up at all. Her blue eyes stood out amongst her pale skin. She wore a grey sweater and black yoga pants. The more he looked at her, the more familiar she became in his mind.

Adam followed Wendy. He couldn't help but feel worried that he would end up in the same disoriented state as his father did after coming here.

There was no backing out now though. Well, there was…but he felt as though he was already too far in.

Wendy led him down a short corridor of 3 or 4 rooms on either side all the way to the last room on the left. She pulled out a key attached to a cord that said "6" and fumbled it in the lock. A click sent the door open to a room that was, again, similar to the rest of the house in that it was adorned with striped wallpaper and a maroon rug. Wendy rolled the small luggage in and parked it next to the bed.

"You're a quiet one, huh? Well you must be beat. Laundry is done every Monday morning. Need anything done - our service will get it done for you. Just make sure to keep windows closed at all times. We don't want any nasty critters in here. Anything else you may need? Oh yeah, breakfast is between 8-10. Before that time, choose a piece of fruit. They're always in the main lobby at the desk.

Adam nodded, "Thank you so much. I had no idea that my father stayed here. It's surreal to be coming back to the same place he was."

Wendy came close to him and gave him an unexpected hug. "Consider us family. Hey, don't be alarmed you may run into my daughter at some point, Sally. She helps with maintenance around here." She headed out of the room.

"Sure thing. Sounds good." Adam nodded in agreement and walked towards the bed. He dropped his other luggage down and waited for Wendy to leave when he finally let himself sink down

53

into the bed. He still couldn't help but feel in his gut that he made the wrong decision to come here.

It was around 7:00 in the evening and his stomach gurgled so he finally sat up on the bed and opened up his phone to search through the nearby restaurants. After scrolling through, his stomach grew more and more impatient and he decided to settle on pizza. Couldn't go wrong with that choice. He dialed the number and was instantly met by a busy tone. He waited and searched for the TV remote.

"Hello, Frank's Pizza. How many I help you?" A girl that sounded like she was just a teenager answered.

It took Adam a moment to answer as he had been distracted looking through the drawers.

"Yeah, I'd like a small cheese pizza with bacon. That's it. Oh - a coke on the side please. I'm at the bed and breakfast on Melbourne Ave. Adam."

"Sure thing. Just give us like 30 minutes. We'll be right there."

She hung up and Adam still had the phone pressed between his shoulder and ear. He let it fall to the ground as he continued to search through the room. He got to the bottom drawer and still nothing. So he made his way to the nightstand, wondering why he didn't just look there in the first place.

Adam sat at the edge of the bed's side and opened the drawer. The remote laid inside rested on a bible with little bits of paper sticking out of it as if they had all just been stashed away there at random. He removed the remote, suddenly disinterested in watching a show as his attention went to the scraps of paper. He picked up the book and started flipping through. Each little bit of paper was folded up and crumpled. He flipped through the first section and it looked as though there was water damage on some of the pages. The Bible's words were underlined and highlighted on the various verses.

Pulling out one piece of paper, he unfolded it and realized his dad's writing.

A persistent knock came at the door.

Messages

7

Startled from his father's writing, he had

forgotten all about the pizza. He jumped up and

opened the door expecting to find Wendy, but

instead found a much younger version.

"Sally?" He guessed. Although her face

resembled Wendy's, she had deep brown hair tied

to the side in a long braid. Her skin was covered in

freckles and she had a pale white face beneath all of

them. What stood out the most to Adam were her

crystal blue eyes that seemed to look straight

through him. Much like Wendy, she had a short,

button-like nose and perked, pink lips. She was wearing a black jumper and held out the pizza.

"How'd you know? Yep, that's me. Well, here's your pizza. It was waiting on the front desk for a little while. Didn't want it to get cold." She handed him the box.

"Thanks! It's nice to meet you." Adam was ready to retreat back to his bed and become a hermit for the remainder of the night. Sally appeared to have other plans in mind. She stood in the doorway and peered in, standing on her tip toes to look over his shoulder towards the bed.

"Ah, I left that in there for you. It didn't take long for you to find it, huh?" She made her way in and picked up the Bible that he had just been looking through.

Adam smirked at what was happening. Make your way in, why don't you…it was amusing how she welcomed herself in. He decided against saying anything as it wasn't his place. Or was it? This was his room that he was renting out. She was already sitting at the edge of the bed, flipping through the Bible. He sat beside her.

"Your father was very religious. Towards the end, he relied heavily on this to help him get by. He felt haunted." It looked as though she reached the page that she was searching for.

"Here." She handed it over and pointed to the folded piece of paper. Adam took it out and unfolded it several times, revealing an entire page of his father's writing.

October 17, 1992

Today, they followed me up to the gate. At that point I left. Adam ran down the boardwalk, scared for his life. Lady made me promise to come back at another time with him. I refused to bring him back. I never saw her look so mad before. But, I couldn't do it. We barely made it out of there before the path closed for good that night. I always went there with more than enough time, but that was lost as soon as I got on the island. All thoughts were always submerged with wonders of the island. And for this too, I can't bring him back. My mind would be too distracted to care for him. As soon as I got home, Adam was tucked away and I viewed the pictures. There were shots from the sunrise earlier that day that I envied to see at all times. If we could always see beautiful things like the sunset, it wouldn't be as valuable to us. I need to remind myself of the importance of nothing being everlasting. I kept scrolling and at night, I had taken pictures of Adam. The first few were illuminated by his bright smile. It soon faded to a look of absolute fear as a figure crouched over him with their hand rested on his shoulder. This is the last time I'll bring Adam here. From now on, I will keep him out of my assignments. Especially to this place. Wendy can care for him. She has a daughter...Sally. She's around the same age. They'll play. Well, I am feeling very spooked by what I have found, but exhausted. I can't find much more energy in myself to continue writing.

Take this as my solemn promise to never bring him back here again.

Adam sat there, shocked. Part of him wanted to believe what his father wrote, but towards the end - no one really believed a word he said. Especially if it was about the paranormal.

"I don't remember this at all," he said, falling back onto the bed - defeated.

Sally moved beside him and turned towards him, "It is spooky. I barely go out there and I am 5 minutes away. I can't imagine what it did to your father going there time and time again. Always wondered what kept him going back."

Adam rubbed his eyes, "What am I doing? I'm falling into the same trap my father did." He got up and started repacking his things. "I can't do this."

He hadn't placed one shirt in his luggage and Sally already grabbed it from his hands.

"Ok. You can go and find another job and spend the rest of your life wondering what if or you can explore your father's work and maybe find out some truths within it." They locked eyes as he weighed his options.

She seemed to read his mind as to what choice he was leaning towards.

"I can come with you if you don't want to go alone."

Lady

8

There was a brief silence in the room that was interrupted by the quiet whisper of the wind. It gently blew the ivory curtains away, exposing the windows. The breeze moved throughout the room in a slow and tender manner. As if it had fingertips, it touched Adam's loose hair and caressed its cold fingers throughout. Adam smiled in his sleep, thinking of when his mother would brush his hair when he was just a child. The chilling aura made its way down his face and outlined his lips.

When the chill traveled down his body, he awoke, confused. Adam must have fallen asleep shortly after Sally and him went through the journal entries. He looked over to the window and saw that it was partially open. It took him a moment to get himself up as the stress of what was to come made him feel more tired than he'd ever felt before. Adam remembered what Wendy had told him about keeping the windows closed and could have sworn he kept it shut the entire night. He reluctantly lifted himself up and off the bed in slow movements and walked over to the window, cranking it closed with the metal latch.

He peered out the window and saw an emptiness outside that he could relate to as he too felt quite hollow. Darkness still enveloped the night sky in an eerie embrace. Adam could see his breath as it fogged up the window since he was so close. He sleepily rubbed his hand against the murky glass and jumped back. He could see his own reflection, but that is not what shocked him. It was the figure outlined to his right in the glass. His palms grew sweaty and his body froze in a paralyzing fear. Because it was dark, he couldn't make out the face, but he knew from the outline of the hair in the bun and dress buttoned all the way up to her neck, that it was the woman from the elevator.

He squeezed his eyes shut and reopened them, hoping to wake from the nightmare. He was still there and could see the figure moving from the window's reflection. He turned around and faced her. Except this time instead of looking down as she had been in the elevator, she was staring right at him with a horrifying smile across her face.

In a matter of seconds, the woman vanished from view and he knew he wanted to remember her face. He went over to his bag and pulled out his sketchbook, flicking the light on. He sat up against the end of the bed and quickly sketched out her oval-shaped face in light strokes and added darker strokes at the top of her head. The strands of hair met at the center in a clean bun with no strands hanging out. Her face was the most difficult to portray as her eyes were quite small but had a stone-like gaze to them. He decided to shade in the area around her pupils with a dark grey tone leaving

the whites of her eyes bare. The last part was her

smile. This wasn't a smile that showed one's teeth in

a happy way. Instead, it was a smirk with her lips

pressed together just as he had seen in the window.

Sandy Shores

9

Adam found himself in bed as his alarm went off. He felt as though he hadn't slept a wink but was relieved knowing that it had all just been a nightmare. He reached over to his phone and clicked the side, silencing its alarm. When he rolled out of bed, he felt a hard book under him that he must've fallen asleep on. It was his sketchbook and was open to a sketch of Lady that had been in his "nightmare." How did a sketch from a dream that he had appear in real life? He immediately closed the book and raced over to the bathroom to splash cold water in his face. He couldn't fall down that same rabbit hole that his dad did. He'd decided to go to the island that day to begin his assignment.

He was able to, once again, snap himself out of the distractions and focus on the purpose for him being there: bird pictures. He laughed to himself when he thought of that as it seemed so silly to just go and take pictures of a bunch of birds. And on top of that, he was getting paid to do so. But it was actually quite an art because it took a lot to catch the birds at the right angle and the best pictures were mid-flight just as they were taking off from the ground. He wanted to go before sunrise to make sure that he could go alone. Although it may have been a better idea to go with Sally and take her up on the offer, he felt sorry to drag her into it.

He knew he'd always wonder if he didn't take the opportunity. He put on a t-shirt and shorts. Looking at the mirror, he was reminded of shaving and sighed as he wished to already be on the road by then. He took the straight razor and began shaving, mind wandering to Sally. He felt such a closeness to her last night that he hadn't felt in years. They were complete strangers but felt as though they had talked all the time. After a few relationships and flings in high school, Adam really just kept to himself. There was always a disconnect with girls he dated. It wasn't anything necessarily wrong, but just because he hadn't met "the one" and kind of accepted that he may never. He immersed himself in his work as that was all he knew.

He splashed cold water onto his face to remove any shaving cream and rechecked his camera equipment. He had everything he needed. The time read 6:08am. He quietly crept out of his room and grabbed a banana from the fruit basket on the front desk to take on the road with him. It was a short drive as Sally had said. Just 5 minutes. Low tide would be at 6:25 and at that point, he had to rush because the pathway to the island would disappear. His window was short and it stressed him out quite a lot, but also challenged him and kept him on his toes.

Parking was completely open, not one car was in the lot. He parked a little closer to the bridge to walk to the beach. His camera bag fit perfectly around his neck and he headed down the bridge. An eerie silence enveloped the air with a hush as the sound of waves crashing came up from the depths of the silence. A small blackbird with an orange patch on its underbelly stood perched atop the railing that outlined the bridge. Adam slowly withdrew his camera and turned it on, selecting focus settings. Waiting patiently for the bird to turn so he could get more shots, he changed the shutter and snapped at least 20 photos of every little movement shift the little bird made.

A screaming child ran up to the now frightened bird and scared him away. Off the bird went, quickly extending its wings and taking off in the distance.

The boy's mother ran over to him and grabbed his hand, bright red, and apologetically said, "I am so sorry!" Then she turned to the boy with a completely different attitude. "That's it! Now you gotta hold my hand if you want to stay here!"

Adam stifled his laughs and tried to look away so the boy wouldn't see him smiling. He faintly remembered his own mother from this. For a moment, his mind took him back to when he had long hair and he would go to the beach with her. In fact, this was the beach that they often went to. Adam's mother brought a wagon to pull him along when he was very young and it was overflowing with sand buckets and other toys to build castles. She was smart to bring so many things to keep him occupied and out of trouble. Whenever they went to the beach, mom wore a large hat that had a black ribbon around it and a bow in the back. Her face was mostly covered up by sunglasses, but always had dark-red lipstick on, even though they were going to the beach. That was just her signature look, he guessed. He kept his backpack in the wagon with him and it held his sketchbooks. His mother was the one that taught him to draw. She too had a backpack around her shoulders that had adult-version sketchbooks at the time.

For some reason, Mr. Moor wasn't usually present during these times. It was almost as if his parents were divorced or separated early on. He just remembers him and his mother - no father present until she wasn't in the picture any longer. Knowing him, he was usually immersed in his work which is what Adam had become like despite all of his attempts not to.

He continued on and came to the end of the bridge, seeing the island. It was low tide which is what he woke up so early for. Ahead, he could see the rocky causeway that opened up right to the island.

Poquahaug

10

Adam was very eager to get to the island already. It took a long time to walk the path. He noticed that many of the trees around the island's perimeter were just like large, bare twigs. There wasn't a single leaf on either of them even though it was in the middle of Summer.

Waves crashed against the path that he walked on. He was worried that he was running out of time before the path would be completely washed away. He hurried up and picked up the pace, almost jogging towards the island. His camera bag bounced up and down against his chest, making his heartbeat faster than before.

He knew much of the history here. From all of the stories that his dad told him (partly true/partly make-believe) and studies he did growing up, he learned that the Natives used the island for spirituality and religious purposes. Its original name was Poquahaug which meant cleared land. When European settlers came and took their land away, the Paugussett tribe cursed the land. Nevertheless, a rich settler's daughter had run the resort that her family built - that was Lady Angeline from the portrait that he broke in his father's office. Lady Angeline had added on a swimming pool, aquarium, bowling alley and a lot of other activities for vacationers. In fact, the aquarium was the largest in the country at that time. Her story seemed very short, but no one was able to find Angeline after the hotel had mysteriously burnt to the ground after the Civil War. The last they knew of her was the newspaper page of Mr. Moor's finding of the portrait.

Adam took one step on the island and heard birds chattering over him as they soared and circled around. He immediately pulled out his camera and got to work. He was able to zoom in and capture the birds. One of them that was completely white (odd for a seagull as they usually had a bit of grey on them in the least) dove down from the sky and into the water, coming up the next minute with a fish.

The others soared after that bird in the air; trying to steal his catch.

This reminded Adam of people that he met throughout college and it was also why he stayed to himself most of the time. Many of the projects would always have at least one person doing much of the work whereas others would leach off of that person's work and get the A, stealing that person's catch. He thought it was unfair and it aggravated the living hell out of him. Whenever possible, he worked alone and didn't mind it at all. The same would happen with upscale jobs. When his father first started as a photographer, he had an award-winning photograph that was actually used by someone else and entered into a contest where they won thousands of dollars. His father couldn't do much because the camera had been stolen without any copyright on the pictures whatsoever. He never got over that.

After many of the photos were taken, he made his way towards the back of the island. The front had a fence so he could not enter. He decided to go around and found part of the fence bent open. There were several sharp pieces of fence sticking out as it looked like it was cut open and broken into. He carefully ducked in and made his way through the opening.

There was an abundance of trees here - it was like a forest and no longer an island. As he walked through, he noticed that there were no squirrels or other little creatures at all. Thick pricker bushes blocked his path towards the middle. He continued to go around and found the smallest of clearings without any trees or grass. Just bare ground. This is what the Native Americans likely referred to when they first named the island Poquahaug, which meant cleared land.

He walked around the clearing, distracted by birds that caught his attention in the sky. The white bird circled the top and the others followed possibly thinking he still had the fish, which had to be devoured by now. Adam caught several more pictures, snapping the camera again and again as the shutter caught 20-30 shots at a time, catching every little movement. The zoom on his camera allowed him to bring the pictures close enough in view so that the birds unique features were more recognizable.

Adam continued on throughout the island and was surprised to hear panting over to his right. He looked over and went towards the sound to find that white bird that he just caught so many pictures of. He no longer looked like the leader of the pack. It laid on its side, catching his last few breaths. A few other birds stood around him and pecked at his limp body after he took his final gulp of air. The red-winged blackbird from earlier had appeared on the branch nearby. It seemed as if he was giving Adam a warning as he looked straight towards him and flew back towards the mainland.

Adam couldn't stand to watch the demise of the white bird any longer and made his way back to the perimeter of the island to head back home. He felt that was enough pictures for that day. He wanted to use the rest of his time sketching at the beach on the mainland.

Flashbacks

11

The weather was perfect after low tide had come and gone. Although higher tides were coming in, the sun remained and its warmth resonated beyond its touch on Adam's skin. Adam wore swim shorts and a t-shirt knowing that he would most likely stay at the beach for a while after. He walked over towards the water but made sure not to be so close as he didn't want his things washed away in case he'd fall asleep. After finding an open spot near the no lifeguard flag, he took his backpack off and laid out the towel that was inside.

At first, he sat on it and pulled out his sketchbook, pondering what to draw first. His thoughts kept bringing him back to the white seagull who had lost his life too quickly. He would draw him.

Adam was never good with blood and gore. He was one of those people that would walk out of the room whenever someone put on a bloody, horror movie at a party. If someone was hurt, he always tried to move past his fears and help them. The bird was unable to be helped at that point as the others had already started to devour him. What had killed him in the first place? Was it the other bird that wanted his fish? That was very strange for seagulls.

After a while of drawing the seagull, he flipped to the next page in his sketchbook and drew the first bird that he captured pictures of – the red-winged blackbird. The image that he wanted to sketch was when he was first lifting off from the ground and soaring up into the air, extending his wings out as far as they could go. Although small, your eye just couldn't miss the fiery glow from the reddish orange on each of his dark wings.

Midway through sketching, he decided to rest back on his towel and found himself slowly dozing off. All too soon, he felt a comfort in the waves as his mind flooded with pleasant memories of his mother and him at the beach. It had been early in the day that they all came there one time because his dad wanted to get pictures of the sunrise. Mom packed breakfast sandwiches in a cooler and was all prepared the night before to go together as a family. When they arrived at the beach, his dad went off with his camera to go catch pictures while he and his mother put out beach chairs and towels.

"Mommy, where's daddy?" He'd ask. She would answer him with a reassuring smile and distract him by bringing up another topic.

"Why don't we build some castles? Come on," she'd walk over to the wagon that they brought and take out all of his sandcastle buckets. He was pretty spoiled in this sense since they came here a lot when he was younger. There were several different sizes that he could choose from. He'd bring them all down as close as he could get to the water without being in it. Wet sand always formed the best castles and stayed for longer. As soon as he was immersed in his sandcastle projects, mom would have already retrieved her sketchbook and she'd be drawing. Much of the time, her drawings were actually of him playing. She loved him more than life itself.

After a while, Adam's father would come back from taking pictures and all Adam could remember was his parents fighting about how long he had been gone. He never saw anyone near his dad but did see him talking quite a lot. Mr. Moor never revealed who he'd been talking to each time.

Awoken

12

Adam began coughing and gasping for air. He realized that he had fallen asleep. His throat was clogged up from some kid nearby that was ignorantly shaking out his towel from all of the sand that it contained.

He looked down at his arms and legs and saw that he started to get a sunburn. There were seagulls near him that must have found his small bag of chips as he no longer had any in his bag. They reminded him of the unfortunate one who was treated much like that bag of chips. He looked down at his watch which probably would make a nice tan line and saw

that it was already past lunchtime. He must have

been asleep for a while. He checked his phone and

saw a message from a number that he didn't

recognize.

10:48am

Hey it's Wendy. Wanna have dinner with us?
We'll be cookin' on the grill out back and would
hate to drive your nose crazy with all the good
cookin'. Much better than ordering pizza again
and again. Just come on back round 5.

He smiled at the text because he had honestly

felt so alone without much of a family anymore.

Wendy made him feel like he was family. He shot back a text.

1:54pm
I'll be there, thanks!

He slid his phone back into his bag and quickly treaded into the shallow waters. He continued to move forward and splashed water onto himself, feeling refreshed. There still weren't many people out here, but he looked toward the island that he ventured out to earlier, wondering what was going through his father's mind whenever he went.

The longer he looked, the more he could tell that there were some people on it. It looked like there were visitors. The path had been washed up, but maybe someone went by boat? No boats around, though… They must've docked in the back of the island or something.

He scratched his head, confused but turned back to gather his belongings and leave so that he could shower and get ready for dinner later.

Reunion

13

The afternoon had flown by since he found himself
preoccupied in his dad's writing although he also
spent a lot of the time looking through his pictures
that he'd taken. He still wanted to go back to the
island to get some more but was too creeped out by
that bird that he left much sooner than he had
hoped to.

The more entries that he found from his father,
the more his interest in exploring more of the island
grew. It was around 4:45 when he decided to head
out back because he could already smell the food

cooking on the grill. On his way out, he passed the kitchen which was actually behind the main lobby and saw Sally preparing some of the sides to bring out. Her hair hung down past her chest and she had a light blue summer dress on with black flip flops. Her skin showed that she was out in the sun a lot more than him as the pale was now lobster red. Adam made a mental note to offer her some of his aloe vera after gel later because boy, he knew that hurt like hell. He walked near her and she was stirring what looked like macaroni salad.

"Hey, want any help?" Adam asked. She looked up and smiled.

"Hey, you're joining us? Yeah, can you bring this outside and just set it on the table? Also some plates and stuff from the cabinets?"

Adam nodded and smiled back. He couldn't help but feel his heart racing in his chest as soon as they came close together. Her understanding about his father and comfort helped him to adjust to this place a lot more.

He took the macaroni salad out of her hands and grabbed some serving spoons from the nearby drawer while he was there then headed outside.

Wendy wore overalls and was cooking on the grill. She looked back at him and smiled, waving over.

"Thought I could help a bit so I came early. It smells so good, thanks for inviting me," he said.

"Oh thank goodness you're here, would you be a doll and cover the grill for me while I run in for a bit?"

He set down everything in his hands on the table and headed over to the grill, taking the spatula out of Wendy's hands. She scuffed up his hair and smiled at him then headed inside. Adam couldn't help but feel that he was just another member of the family to her. She made him feel that he had always been there and wasn't a stranger that just came back. He saw chicken wings and some burger patties on the grill that still needed a few more minutes so he closed the grill.

When he first came here, he didn't notice how big their lot of land was and looked out to see an in-ground pool with a stone patio lined around it. The grill was on a porch that was directly next to the pool. He could see the paint chipping off of the porch, but it was big enough to hold an outdoor table with 6 seats around it.

Wendy had a speaker on the table that played hits from the 70's to 90's; making it quite the eclectic playlist. He didn't mind as he grew up with pretty much the same taste in music from being around his father.

"Hey there, you may want to turn around and check the grill…" Sally came over and burst out laughing when he opened it up to let out a colossal poof of smoke in the air. He quickly turned the heat down a bit and flipped the burger patties and chicken wings onto the plate that Sally held next to him. She couldn't seem to stop laughing, but he felt so bad that he ruined the food.

"Hey, kids!" Wendy said, on her way out again.

"Mom, I hope you wanted these to be extra well-done, because if you did, Adam's got your back!" Sally said and continued smiling on her way over to the table with the blackened food.

We all sat around the table and each had 1 burger and a few chicken wings. The very outside was crisp, but the middle was still edible.

"Hey, it's alright kid. You just made sure to cook off all that bacteria so we don't get sick. So thoughtful of you!" Wendy reassured Adam.

They all laughed and started talking about what their summer plans were. Sally would go onto intern until college started up again while Adam would just be going on assignments from back in the city. He explained that this was his first assignment.

Somehow, the conversation moved to his father and they discussed that Sally and Adam used to always play when they were young kids. The faint memories came back the more they spoke about it.

"So are you spooked out about the island at all? I know your dad was for a long time," Wendy asked. Adam just told them that he had heard about the paranormal activity but didn't believe much of it at all. It was all just ghost stories to keep the tourists out so that the residents of this town wouldn't have too many other people flooding into their beaches.

"Yeah, but you've gotta give it to your father that there's got to be some truths in what he's said over the years. Well, lemme know if you see anything when you're over there. I'm gonna start cleaning up." Sally protested and persisted that her mother go in to rest and that she would take care of the clean-up. It wasn't very hard to talk Wendy out of cleaning everything up as she just went back inside after one request from Sally.

Adam stayed to help her. At one point, they both grabbed the same plate and smiled up at one another. "What're you doing the rest of the night?" He asked.

"Nothing really, why?" She continued piling the dishes up to bring them back inside.

"Well we could watch a movie or something if you want?"

"Yeah, I'd be down."

Close

14

Cleaning had never been more enjoyable when
you're splashing water and making even more of a
mess while you're trying to wash dishes. Adam just
couldn't help it because for some reason, Sally
brought out this silly side of him. He just flicked over
some water her way then she got on the defense
and Adam ended up completely drenched in water.
It took twice as long since they had to mop up the
floor. They agreed to meet up in the lobby after they
changed clothes.

Adam made it back first and started searching through the movies that were stacked up right below the television. For some reason, he felt like watching a horror movie that didn't have blood and gore. The kind of horror movie that was more of a mystery... Or maybe it was because he wanted Sally to get close to him. Either way, he decided on one and pulled it out. As soon as he placed the disc in the DVD player, Sally came over and plopped herself on the couch beside him.

"Sorry it took so long, I had to answer some emails for school," she was in penguin shorts and a white tank top while she sat criss-cross on the couch. Adam had to force himself to look away because he couldn't help but smile at how cute she looked.

They sat back and watched the movie. Around 30 or so minutes in, Sally rested her head on his shoulder. This made him feel like he had a purpose and he wrapped his arm around her. She started talking about the journal entries from his dad and their conversation became far more important than any movie as it was now just background noise.

"Have you found anything else in his writing?" She asked.

"Nah, but I've been having some weird dreams about the things that I've been reading. One of the dreams is about that woman that he keeps referring to – Lady Angeline," he said, looking down at his feet, surprised that he had brought her up.

"Well, we should keep looking through that book. I can help you if you want?" she persisted.

They left the movie playing in the lobby and headed back over to his room. As soon as he pulled out the book from the nightstand, he turned around and saw Sally come close up to him, so close that their lips touched. He set down the book on the nightstand behind him.

Sally pushed him to sit down on the the edge of the bed and she kissed him with what felt like all of her strength as it was hard to stay sitting and not be pressed down onto the bed. He wrapped his arms around her as they continued kissing repeatedly, preoccupied in one another's presence.

"I don't know what it is about you, Adam," Sally said between the breaths that she took from kissing him, "but I really like you a lot."

This time, Adam pushed her back onto the bed and continued kissing her back, passionately. They heard a few footsteps from out in the hallway and stopped, abruptly. Wendy must have heard them. Sally put her finger in front of her lips and it was hard not to chuckle as they played this childish game of hide and seek from Sally's own mother. After a few minutes, they took a sigh of relief realizing they were in the safe zone and weren't caught.

"Wanna watch somethin'," Sally brought out the remote for the TV. Adam nodded, putting his arm around her and allowed himself to relax back into

the bed.

Clearing

15

When Adam woke up the next morning, he saw that Sally still laid in the bed next to him and smiled at her. He slowly crept out of bed so that he could go back to the island to take more pictures. For some reason, he felt weird just leaving and decided to write a note to her.

Sally,

I had a good time with you last night. Another movie tonight and this time let's try to watch it? Or not, up to you, I don't mind either way. I didn't want you to think that I was leaving without saying anything — I'm headed back to the island for some more pictures. I'll be back later. Looking forward to seeing you again.

Adam.

He set the note on top of her phone, which was on the nightstand. That would be a place that she would surely look. When he grabbed his camera from the office, he realized his sketchbook was there next to it and open. His heart sank when he realized what the sketch was – Lady. It was of Lady Angeline from the dream that he had or thought he had...

He closed the page, wishing to banish that page from existence and headed out, hoping that he could take Sally with him but not having the heart to wake her up when she looked so calm and at peace.

This time, he headed to the island shortly after 7am and knew it would still be low tide because that's when he planned to come the night before. There were a few more people in the parking lot this time. He went on his way, snapping pictures of the birds that he passed by when he headed towards the island.

Again, the red-winged blackbird met him on that bridge that connected the parking lot with the beach. When he continued on, the bird extended its wings and flew in front of him. He stopped and looked over at it, but kept going. The bird did this once more as if to stop him from continuing towards the island, but he ignored it.

The causeway appeared and he followed it down to the island then went around back and through the bent fence, which he used the time before to make his way into the center clearing of the island. Historians had said that the hotel was in the direct center and after it burnt down, nothing else grew at all. This is where the clearing seemed to be.

As he walked towards it, the sound of waves slowly dissipated until there was no sound at all. Adam felt like he had stepped into another dimension. His mind went blank and body numb. He closed his eyes and tried to imagine his dad when he had visited all of those times.

In his dad's writing, he remembered another note that mentioned the clearing in the center and said to be weary of the trance-like state that it could leave you in. Adam wasn't quite sure what that meant though.

He stood up and exited the clearing. As soon as he did that, he felt his heart stop as the world around him had changed in some way. There were still trees around and grass… well, minus the clearing, but the sky above darkened. He was so confused. A storm? He checked the forecast and there was no prediction of storms that day. He looked down at his watch and it read 6:00pm. Impossible. Someone was playing a prank. But how?

Time Change

16

When Adam checked his watch, he could have sworn only minutes passed by. The sky, suddenly dark, told him that it had to be a storm. But his watch said otherwise. How long had he been there? How was this possible? He tried to make his way towards the shore of the island, recalling the path he took there was faded from his memory. Aside from the clearing, were far more pricker bushes than he noticed before. They stood in his way of reaching the deep forest.

Adam looked around at all of the pricker bushes. He discovered a large stick that he picked up and attempted making a path, smushing them down. He only managed to push them down by a few inches when he grew tired and impatient, stepping on the bushes instead. His shoes were not the best, some sliced through his left shoe, piercing the sole of his foot. He winced. It took about 6 or 7 painful steps for him to reach the end of the agonizing prickers.

He sat down in the grass next to them and slowly took off his shoes. As he peeled them off, he felt the spikes press into his feet that much more. He knew he had to take them off, though. Walking would only cause more pain. He saw them protruding through his socks on both feet and took each out, one by one. After he finished, he sat there staring up at the sky in pain. Being in the city, he'd been used to light pollution's effect on the sky. This was very different…he could actually see several stars shining bright and noticed the moon. Then, it struck him.

Night.

He somehow arrived early in the morning and was still there with the moon out. He was there all day. It puzzled him that he felt like he was there for just a mere hour or two. None of it made any sense. He looked down at his watch, which was now glowing - 10:46pm. He had no idea what was happening, but had to get out of there, quickly. He grabbed his socks and shoes and hurried to put them on, not caring anymore about the pain. The rush only seemed to make him go slower...

He stood up and made his way through the forest. There were minimal animals and no birds, but he did see several bats swooping above him. An owl's calls echoed in the distance. Ahead, it looked like there was a narrow path made of dirt. He eagerly followed it, hoping that it would bring him back to the bent fence so he could make his way to the coast again. It stopped short of what looked like a field of tall grass. He suddenly felt a rushing wind blow right through him. It pushed him back a bit and he turned around, looking behind him only to find a person standing about 10 feet away from him. Their face was hidden in the darkness and they stood still as a statue. He felt thankful that there was someone else there at least and he wasn't alone.

"Hey! What're you doing out here? Do you know the way back??" he said as he started to slowly walk toward them.

There was no answer. Just silence.

The tranquility forced him to caution his steps. He paused where he stood and attempted again, "I mean no harm. I just want to know if you know the way back and can help me."

This time, he was met with an answer. The figure lunged towards him. The closer they came, the more recognizable they appeared to him. It was, again, the woman from the elevator and that 'nightmare.' This time, her hair was disheveled and no longer in a bun. She wore the same button down dress to her feet, but it was torn and ripped up in various places. The off-white color that it had been now replaced with a series of tears and brown stains.

Adam turned around and began to run the opposite way. He had no idea what she wanted from him but knew that she was not trying to help and this time, she was chasing him.

He stepped through the tall grasses that extended up to his knees when suddenly, he felt his legs turn to jelly and the rest of his body followed suit as he tumbled down a small embankment. His camera went flying, the flash going off in sporadic clicks for some reason. A giant bulge pressed into his back where he lay. Using his hands, he felt underneath him and its texture was similar to that of

a wooden log. It hurt like hell. He looked all around

him and could see no sign of the woman. If he stood

up, she would surely see him. Laying there, he was

at least hidden by the tall grasses. He debated just

laying there for a few minutes. The energy escaped

him. His feet were a bloody mess - and no not the

English phrase - they were literally seeping blood

through his socks…his back, bruised. The wind was

knocked out of him when he fell. His father warned

him again and again. His curiosity won over any

advice Mr. Moor could have given.

The Natives

17

Adam decided on staying there to recover for a few minutes. It's not like he had much of a choice either. He was no use, stumbling and crawling out of there would take just as long and he would only get more hurt. His fear irked him and it was most troubling to be completely alone in this so late at night. He should have taken Sally up on her offer…

He focused his attention on looking straight up at the night sky. It was a bit of a calm in all of this. The big dipper was directly above where he laid. His eyes followed it as if to trace the outline over and over. His mother taught him that when he got upset and scared whenever they went camping.

He remembered her saying, "And no matter where you are, just remember, we are all under the same sky and will always be. You're not alone."

A strong wind brushed passed his face and made him feel more awake. It gave him the bit of energy that he needed to get himself up. As he sat up, he noticed a woman peering at him from behind a tree. He froze in fear.

She had long, thick black hair that went down to her hips. Red and yellow paint markings were drawn on her face in a tribal design. Her skin looked dark and reddish, but not quite sunburnt. She was wearing a light brown covering unlike clothes he normally saw. She was staring straight at him.

He broke the silence, "Hello?" She quickly moved one finger in front of her mouth, shushing him and crept by his side, kneeling.

The woman leaned her face down towards his ear and whispered, "My people do not want you here on this island. You need to leave."

"I'm try-" he forgot to whisper and she placed her finger in front of his lips. The coldness in her touch shocked him.

Adam remembered to whisper this time, "I'm trying to leave. I am hurt; I can barely get up." His legs ached from the fall.

Whispering didn't seem to matter. Men and women, who wore the same types of coverings as the girl who knelt beside him began appearing from behind the trees. Adam felt her stand up right away and step away from him.

One of the biggest men spoke out to her, but it was in another language so Adam couldn't understand. His hair was long like the woman's, but back in a pony tail. He had similar face paint on, but it extended down his shoulders and arms as well.

As soon as the man finished talking, she replied still in their language. Adam knew they were talking about him because she pointed his way several times. The man nodded his head and put his hand up as if to call other people his way. Four much stockier men full of muscle, but not as tall came over

towards Adam. Two stood on each side then bent

down and picked him up. Adam did not struggle at

all. Something told him to trust this woman. Looking

over his shoulder, he saw her staring at him,

reassuring.

Remedy

18

Listening to her was his best decision since coming to the island. Her people brought him into what looked like their village. It was hard to understand how he didn't pass the village before. It only took a few minutes for them to step foot in the village. The shelters were made from tree bark and looked very similar to that of Native American homes he remembered studying in school. The men that carried him went inside one of the shelters and placed him down upon the ground. They left and coincidentally, another woman appeared through the doorway. She had red and black paint over her entire face, and was carrying a brown bag, which she opened up as she knelt beside him. Unlike the rest of the group, she had green eyes that seemed oddly familiar.

The woman did not say a word. She just reached into the bag and pulled out a bowl and some other items like leaves, a jar of lavender and jug of water. She placed a little of each into the wooden bowl and used a rock to mash the items before dunking her fingers in and spreading the mixture on his feet. She turned him over and put the same on his back, too. It felt like a cooling gel - similar to aloe vera that his mother used to put on him after he got too sunburnt. He strained to get up and she gently pushed him down again.

"Leave it for a little," she said. He obeyed. Her voice sounded strikingly similar. He knew not to question it though, so he just laid there. His back felt much better and his feet were numb, he had to lift his head up to make sure they were still there.

The woman walked away and came back with a rag. She dipped it into the water and began wiping her face paint off for some unknown reason. At first, the red and black smeared all towards one spot - but eventually, she was able to completely wipe the paint off.

Adam felt bad staring at her so he wasn't looking her way and instead, off to the lavender jar - deep in thought. He felt so tired and thought maybe he could use a nap. What a silly idea. He had no idea where he was and who he was with and he was going to nap? But he was just so tired…

Right before he felt his eyes closing, his blurred vision revealed the woman without any face paint on. It was his mother.

Gone

19

Adam found himself at the entrance of the pathway

back towards the beach. He was laying in the sand

and felt as if nothing happened. He got up and his

feet were no longer sore; neither was his back. He

looked at the island and then back to the coast. The

pathway was revealed so he had time to make his

way back. He checked his watch and it showed

6:45am. That was around the time he just got to the

island to begin with. He must have fallen and hit his

head or something. Did he have a dream? He swore

it was real. The last time he thought it was just a

dream, he found that sketchbook with a drawing that he made from the supposed nightmare. Why was his mother on this island and why did she leave him and his father? The time change made no sense either.

He started walking down the causeway and at that time, there were a few more people on the beach than before. Mostly retired folks were going on their morning walks and the waves were quite calm and peaceful at low tide.

They waved over to him when he passed by, but he was very distracted by his own thoughts. He felt so spooked and was shaking but walked down the bridge after he got past the coast and saw the same black bird looking at him. He went to reach for his camera only to realize that it was gone - there was nothing around his neck - no camera bag, no camera. He must have left it on the island.

There was no way that he was going to head back there and besides, low tide was coming to an end and the pathway was probably already washed up. It did upset him deeply because that was one of his most prized possessions that his father passed down to him. He planned on never going back and turning down the assignment, even if it meant losing the job completely. But, he had to get the camera. That went without question.

When he finally reached his car, he sunk down into the seat, defeated. After about 15 minutes of sitting down in silence, hearing more cars coming into park, he turned the keys in the ignition - feeling

lucky to still have that at the very least and headed

back to Wendy's.

Maria

20

He managed to get to his room without running into Wendy or Sally. They were both probably out somewhere. He looked over at the nightstand to see that Sally had taken the note and her phone. It was just about to be 8 in the morning. He laid in his bed and tried to go back to sleep. That would have been nice anyway.

After a while, he realized that it would be impossible to fall back to sleep after the morning he had. There was just no way that he'd forget that. And even better, no one would believe him. He was just like his father. In such a short time, too, he was lost. His mind was lost to the wonder that the island stood for; that he was warned about time and time again.

He pulled the Bible out of the nightstand and began flipping through its pages. There were so many folded up scraps of paper that he could choose from. He just wanted answers but wasn't sure if he would find them. Reading his father's notes would probably leave him with more questions.

He decided to keep searching anyway.

On the page after the one that Sally showed him was a pink folded paper that he gently unfolded, worried that he would break it apart.

October 18, 1993

I keep telling myself that I will not come back to the island. I try to convince myself and always fail. I stopped bringing Adam with me, so I guess that's a start. It was hard never bringing him back because I know he wants to see his mother. He always asks about her. "Where'd mommy go? I miss her so much." It breaks my heart, but I tell him that she's on vacation. I don't like lying to him, but it's better than the truth.

Wendy has been so good to him. She watches him and has been understanding. I always tell her that I have to go back to the island for work, but I know that she can see through it.

Today is October 17, 1993. It marks 3 years since we have last seen Maria.

Adam felt reluctant to continue reading because his gut was once again right, he was only left with more questions after reading more of his father's entries. He had just felt himself drifting in and out of sleep when he heard a knock on the door.

He sat up on the bed,

"Yeah, come in."

Normality

21

It was Sally. She wore a bright yellow dress that turned his mood around in an instant. Her wavy brown hair hung down to the bottom of her chest. She had no mascara or any form of makeup on similar to her mother. She stayed in the doorway when speaking to him this time. He guessed that she could probably tell he looked disheveled. She had no idea…But right now, he felt the urge to get up and press her against the wall, kissing her again and again as he had the other night.

"If you're not too tired, wanna come grab some brunch with me? If not, it's cool. Gonna head over to the deli and grab a few sandwiches. They've got a huge picnic area to eat at."

He hesitated as he tried to come up with an excuse not to, but then thought it would actually be good to get out and do something semi-normal in the craziness that his life had become.

"Yeah, that actually sounds good. I'll meet you in the lobby," he got up and headed towards the bathroom to freshen up. He was glad to have Sally to keep him occupied. For all he knew, he would just continue to read through his father's notes and get more and more curious to go back to the island, which he needed to do anyway to retrieve the camera.

After a few minutes, he found himself in the lobby, waiting. Wendy came out and said, "Hey Sally told me you guys were getting brunch. Sounds good! I'd come but I've gotta take care of some things over here."

"Yeah, she just invited me! I got a few pictures this morning already, but I'm gonna head back tomorrow. Gotta wait till low tide." Adam replied then sat down in the chair and picked up a magazine to read as he waited.

"What're you waiting for? She's right out front in her car, you goof!" Wendy said as Adam felt his cheeks grow red and flush. He waved goodbye and she blew him a kiss. Strange to him. He just awkwardly continued waving as he headed out the door and got into Sally's car.

"Took you long enough!" She said and before he could reply she connected her phone to the car to play her music. The first song that her playlist shuffled to was one of Elvis Presley's. Adam took a mental note of this as she was quite eccentric like him.

"So, let's go to the deli and get some sandwiches. We can eat there, but I've got mom's order and we can bring one back for her too. You have anything else planned today? Low tide isn't till around 2 in the morning so I'm guessing work is out of the question."

Adam leaned back in his seat, making himself comfortable as he took in all the familiar places that Sally zoomed by in her car. Memories flooded back in his mind from his visits as a child.

"Not much planned, actually."

Sally pulled into a parking lot at a Deli place called, "Rosa's Deli."

"That's good, we don't have to rush then. Come on, I'll tell you some of the good sandwiches they've got." We both got out of the car and walked in. Sally talked the whole way in and during their time in line about the different sandwiches they had. He decided to get the same thing that she was ordering - The Florence. This had chicken cutlet, cheddar cheese, bacon, lettuce and tomato. They ordered it on a sub. It sounded really good by how Sally described it, so he took her word for it. He was sold at the mention of bacon.

When they got to the counter, Sally ordered for both of them. The man behind the counter looked very happy to be there. He also seemed to run the place.

"Hey Sally, who's this young guy you've brought in? A boyfriend?" he asked, looking straight at Adam.

"Oh, this is Adam! Do you remember him from when we were young? With Mr. Moor?"

It didn't even take one more moment for him to come around from behind the counter and embrace Adam in a big hug. "Look at you! You've grown so big, I couldn't recognize you!! Welcome back! On the house today, guys!" he yelled back towards the workers behind the counter. Adam couldn't have felt more awkward, but he just went along with their joy,

"It's so nice to see you, and it's good to be back!" He went on to tell him about why he was back as he flooded him with several questions. Sally smiled at him the whole time as she seemed to get a kick out of this.

On Board

22

It took quite a while to finally get out of the deli, but time went by fast since their sandwiches were ready before they were done talking. Adam didn't mind too much. It took his thoughts to another place; giving him the distraction that he needed.

They walked outside and went around back to sit at a picnic table. It was a beautiful day out.

"So what do you do?" Adam asked Sally. She finished chewing the last bite she took.

"Well, I'm helping mom out, but I take courses online for college. I'm trying to go into writing. I'm supposed to intern this summer at a publishing company, but we'll see how that works out."

"Oh that's really neat, we need more writers around. What kind of writer are you trying to be?" Adam continued eating his sandwich, glad he chose it as it was just as delicious as Sally described.

Sally looked off in the distance. "I am actually really interested in writing mysteries. I read them all the time and I guess your father's stories of the island got me into all that paranormal spooky stuff."

He gulped down his food. He wanted to tell Sally about what happened but was scared that she wouldn't talk to him any longer. But she said herself that she listened to his father. He decided against it.

"Oh that's cool, do you believe in any of the stuff he said?" Adam genuinely wanted to know.

"I believe in some of it. It really depends. One of the biggest things that I honestly believe to be true is that no one is truly ever gone. There are so many crazy stories out there, yes. But science proves that one to be a fact.

"Did something happen when you went to the island this morning?"

Adam felt his heart sink in his chest. Should he just tell her? Tell her everything that happened? What did he have to lose??

"Just got a few pictures. I have to go back and pick up the camera," he shrugged.

They sat in silence for a few minutes. Sally crossed her arms and Adam could tell that she knew he was leaving out something. He decided to tell her everything from the moment he saw the black bird on the boardwalk to when he woke up on the sandy shore of the island.

The entire time, she nodded her head and didn't even stop to take one bite of her sandwich. He had her full attention, which was surprising considering how much of a lunatic he sounded like. As soon as he was done telling her what happened, he looked down at his sandwich, embarrassed.

"Well, there's only one thing to do. Let's go back there and get your camera."

Searching

23

When they got back from Rosa's Deli, they had both agreed to look through Mr. Moor's entries to find out more about what he saw going to the island each time. They planned to go at low tide, but this time it was around 2 in the morning. Adam tried to talk Sally out of it and persisted that she should just stay home while he went because it wasn't safe for her. He found that there was no talking Sally out of this, though.

She flipped through several notes from within the Bible and they decided that each note should be placed back in its original placement in the Bible as the various entries could have some connection to where they were placed.

"You find anything about my mother, Maria?" Adam asked Sally as he continued reading through one of the scraps of paper.

"Nah, not yet. Just some more visits to the island by himself and this lady he saw a lot named Angeline," she replied, still looking down and reading.

"Does he describe what she looks like-" Adam asked, pausing for a moment. "Does she have a bun and a button-down dress to her feet?" He continued.

Sally stopped cold in her tracks and put the paper down, looking over to Adam. It took her a moment to answer this, but she said "Yes…is that the Lady that you saw when you were there?"

Adam nodded as Sally handed him the paper that she had been reading.

October 18, 1995

Every time I go to the island, I am haunted by her. From the moment I come here to sleep and through nightmares and dreams, she comes. She lurks within my mind and refuses to leave. I go to the island and I see her, unable to find Maria because she has chased me away. I realized she has trapped them in a way because no one is able to get out and they can only stay within.

It is a strange phenomenon. Lives that are lost there seem to stay there. And this is why I come back — to be with Maria.

I bring her photos of our son and things that he has made for her because she begs me to. Even if I cannot make it to her, I leave them by the clearing hoping they will get to her.

I now have scars all over my body from the Lady sinking her teeth into my flesh and the many, many times she has caused me to fall.

To her, this is her island. She is the only one to say who stays and goes because she has forever been cursed by the Natives for building on their sacred soil.

Adam stood up after reading the note right away. He placed his hands on Sally's shoulders. "This is who I saw that morning, Sally. The same thing has been happening to me here; I am having night terrors whenever I sleep and she's been in every single one of them."

She got up and stared back into his eyes. "Why don't we get some sleep before we go there, hm?" Sally didn't know what else to say to him. She feared that he was, in fact, falling down the same path that his father had. She remembered the days that Mr. Moor was there while his son was at college, safe. Mr. Moor would be gone for days at a time and come back looking as if he had run a marathon and fallen into mud again and again. Her mother would question it, but Mr. Moor just simply shrugged it off and would go back into his room where he asked not to be disturbed. Sally decided to go with Adam to see if there were any truths to what he had been saying, but the frequent dreams only reminded her of Mr. Moor.

She would go get his camera without him, giving

him no reason to go back to the island.

Alone

24

Somehow, Sally was able to talk Adam into resting. It didn't take very long and was almost as if he hadn't gotten any sleep the night before since he fell right to sleep almost as soon as his head hit the pillow. She stayed there a while ensuring that he was fast asleep before she left.

He laid back and still had his shoes on, but this was the first time she saw him look as though he was at peace and calm. She laid back, plotting her journey to the island that she honestly refused to go to because of how creepy it was. The last time she went was when she was still in high school and a group of kids thought it would be cool to go at night. Most of them made it only halfway down the causeway before chickening out. Another time she went with a friend, they followed the path all the way down and any little sound spooked them.

This time would be different, though, because she would be going alone.

Nighttime fell and the hours dragged on, but the clock finally turned to 1:30am and Sally crept out of Adam's room, closing the door quietly behind her.

As she assumed, there were not many people on the road on her way to the parking lot of the beach. She pulled up to the closest space to the bridge since every space was bare and open.

The night sky around was only illuminated by the full moon, which seemed two times larger than it normally appeared. The bridge that took her from the parking lot to the shore was over a swamp, but since it was low tide there wasn't much water and only the thick, tall grasses poking out of the ground. Normally, there would be birds flying about but the only sound were crickets all around her. When she neared the end of the bridge, a blackbird – similar to the one that Adam had mentioned, flew right in front of her. It extended its wings and looked as though it may land right on her head. She jumped back but saw the speck of fiery red on its wing fly off into the night.

Sally picked up her pace and made it past the bridge and looked out at the pathway to the island. The pebbles and rocks stretched out and made it appear that it would be an endless journey. The moon illuminated the sky and reflected in the waters. This made her feel more at ease. If it had been a cloudy night, there would be complete darkness.

She reminded herself that all she had to do was retrieve Adam's camera and hurry right back as she did not want to be here for a minute longer than she had to. While on her way, she couldn't help but feel that someone was watching her. Afraid, she didn't want to turn back and continued on in a hurry. Instead of going around the perimeter and through the back, she hopped the fence in the front and began her search for the camera. She turned her phone's light on to help guide her. Adam had described the camera being near a bit of a clearing and somewhat close to tall grasses. Part of her regretted not going with Adam, but she felt it was her job to make sure Adam didn't come back.

The ground was muddy and she tried to keep on the grass so that her shoes would stop sinking in. To her right, was a giant tree that had long spear-like sticks rested against it. These looked man-made and as if someone was trying to make weapons to use as protection.

But who would make them? And why?

There wasn't time to investigate this. She

continued towards the clearing and found the

camera. Surprisingly, there was no mud or any tears

on the case. She picked it up and opened the bag,

turning the camera on. The photo albums of shots

Adam took was quite difficult to find, but she

managed to search her way through the camera to

locate it. He must have clicked the button by

accident because as she scrolled, there were a

series of random shots of trees that looked like he

used the flash to take. He had gone in the morning,

though, which didn't make sense. It was bright and

sunny that day. He shouldn't have had to use it and it

wouldn't be night in the pictures...

When she quickly scrolled through the shots, she passed one in particular that had more than just trees in the image. A woman with messy, brown hair and a torn up dress was in front of the trees and looked as though she was lunging right for Adam. Sally used the zoom to look closer at her. Moving it up to the lady's face, she noticed that she was smiling and headed right for Adam.

Absence

25

Some would say that it was a good idea for Sally to take matters into her own hands and get the camera. But others…well…most, would say that it was the worst idea she had come up with. Shortly after she left, the same dream had come to Adam where the window was open and let in a cool breeze that woke him. This time, he realized it wasn't a dream as he found a note left from Sally that she went off to get his camera without him.

Adam,

I guess this is going to be a thing for us to leave each other notes. I didn't want to wake you either this time and you seemed very traumatized by what happened at the island. So, I thought that I'd just go get your camera and bring it back for you. I'll be back soon if you get this beforehand. You're right, we should watch another movie together. I'm fine with watching it or just keeping it on in the background. You should come visit more often. You're a really cool guy.

Sally

He felt panicked. She had no idea how it truly was when going to the island, especially at night. He checked his watch and it was around 1:55am, which left about 5 minutes until low tide.

He rushed about the room, grabbing his phone, wallet and keys then made his way over to his car.

The drive seemed to take forever even though it was a mere few minutes away to the parking lot. When he finally arrived there, he saw Sally's lone car in the closest spot to the bridge and parked right next to it. As he jumped out of the car, he wasted no time and ran down the bridge.

Why would she go by herself? She had suggested that it would be a good idea to take a nap before going, but never mentioned that she would just take off without him and go. It didn't make any sense. Did she believe him? His mind went right to the lady that had chased him down. He kept hoping that Sally wouldn't run into her when she got the camera.

"Please just let her get the camera and be on her way back," he said to himself while jogging along the bridge.

When he finally made it to the shore, he saw a figure at the end of the path to the island, just stepping foot there. He figured it was her and yelled out, "Sally! Wait up!"

Her

26

The image of the woman spooked Sally so much so that her body went into shock. She felt her palms grow sweaty and couldn't seem to move from the spot that she was standing in. Her curiosity peaked as she continued scrolling through pictures.

As she looked through more and more, she could see the woman getting farther and farther away from Adam. This was because she was going backwards through the photos, so she had really been getting closer to him. The same smile was spread across her face which was bruised and partially burnt. On her right cheek, the flesh was not there much and instead, there were several pink impressions as if the skin had been peeled back.

Was this the lady that he talked about? That visited him in his dreams and was in the elevator that time? What did she want with him?

There was just no explaining this. She looked over at the clearing to her right and wondered why Adam made his way in this far on the island. She decided to go back the way she came and never come here again. Placing the camera back in its case, she put it over her head to hang down from her neck and turned around.

The moon no longer provided light to the night sky. While she looked through the pictures, clouds must have come in and blanketed its light, causing darkness to overwhelm her tremendously with even more of a fear of not being able to make her way back to the mainland.

Crackles in leaves filled her ears in what once was a quiet night other than the wind blowing the trees. The sounds came from all around her, she didn't know where to look first. There was a humming coming from her left and next to the oak tree with the spears stood the lady from the pictures on Adam's camera. She had been watching Sally this whole time.

Untold

27

Adam had finally reached the island after walking its pathway as Sally was unable to hear his shouts to her. He saw that the front fence was bent down as she must have used this to get through to the center. He followed what he thought were her steps and made his way past the tall grasses and towards the oak tree that stood next to the clearing. There was nothing, not even his camera which he could have sworn was right next to the clearing when he last saw it after his fall.

He continued through and made his way to the opposite side where fencing was broken down. This was where he originally entered on his first visit. There was no sign of her. Maybe she already found the camera and then went home? She would be waiting for him in the parking lot because he parked next to her.

This seemed like a pretty good idea so he decided to go through the fence and walk around the island's perimeter back to the front. The moon had come out again as the clouds passed by and the sky was again illuminated much more than it had previously been.

As soon as he got to the front, he saw a girl sitting down on one of the biggest rocks right before the causeway. Her head was down in her hands and she looked as though she was crying. The closer he got, the more he recognized who the girl was. Sally.

He ran up to her and embraced her in a hug. Not sure what happened, but her silent cries were pressed into his shoulder, dampening his shirt.

"Come on, let's leave and go back. We don't have to come here again," he reassured her. He took her hand in his and tried to lead her up so that they could go back across the island. The cold skin of her palms shocked him and looking back at her, he realized that she wore his camera around her neck.

When he tried to lead her to pathway, she planted her feet and refused to go any further.

Adam was puzzled as he thought she wanted to leave. Her face was pale as if she had just seen a ghost and he felt her shaking where she stood. She wasn't looking at Adam, though. Her gaze was right in front of them towards the path.

"What is it?" Adam said before he followed her eyes and saw exactly what it was.

Lady was blocking their path and pacing back and forth at the entrance as if to guard it. Every time she walked towards them; she just smiled their way. They wouldn't be able to get past her.

Sally tugged on Adam's shirt and he lowered his head down. She brought her lips to his ear and whispered to him, "She took me and I was here on this rock. I don't know what happened, I just remembered seeing her and then blacking out. She

told me that we can't leave."

Saved

28

Just then, the lady no longer paced as a spear flew right by her and landed next to her feet. She looked up and smiled as if it meant nothing and could not affect her in any way. She continued pacing, but several more spears flew her way. This seemed to anger her and she ran towards the origin of the many throws.

The woman that Adam had met who appeared to look just like his mother snuck up behind Adam and Sally. She looked as though she was in a hurry.

"Quick - you need to run down the pathway before its too late. We are distracting her. We don't want her to take another life to be trapped here on this island. She has already taken too many. But you must go now. The pathway will never open again after tonight; she will no longer be able to take more."

"Mom?" Adam blurted out. The woman nodded. Her face was adorned in the paint again, but he could still tell it was her by her green eyes that he had, too.

"Yes. I want to be with you, but we can't. I lost my life on this island so I am trapped here as part of the curse so my job is to keep this land sacred with the others."

Adam was reluctant to leave as he had so many more unanswered questions. He longed to just sit with her and talk. Was this why his father was obsessed with the island? So that he could see his mother?

They looked over at the entrance to the path and saw that it was bare and the lady was no longer there so they took this chance and ran for it. Sally went first as Adam remained frozen in place, still in shock. She called back and said, "Come on!!!" Adam turned back to his mother and she hugged him before pushing him to follow Sally. They ran as fast as they possibly could but made sure to keep their hands grasped together so that they didn't lose one another again.

The waves from both sides of the path forced themselves against where they stood, as they already seemed to be concealing the way. Adam peeked behind himself as they ran and saw there was no longer an entrance to the island. Usually, high tide would slowly cover the way but this time it seemed to cease from existence as soon as they made their way through.

When they reached the shore, they both turned around and saw that there was no way back. They turned to one another and held each other. Sally sobbed and buried her face into Adam's shoulder while he peered out to the island, seeing Lady Angeline drag his mother back to the fence. As they walked farther away, they soon became just two

figures then nothing at all as they went out of sight.

After

29

Days had gone by since the incident and Adam and Sally refused to bring it up. The elephant in the room was not just for the sake of one another's protection but also because they didn't want to open a wound that was still healing for each of them.

The tragedy that passed only left them with more questions and more curiosity to someday go back there. But they knew that they had to stay away as the island would be off limits to all for some time. Boats used to be able to dock nearby, but they learned that many spears and rock formations appeared after that day which disabled visitors the entry. It was for the better. Even during low tide, no pathway emerged from the depths of the ocean. All of the rocks seemed to have washed away.

At times, they both found themselves talking a walk at that very beach, looking out at the mystery and getting lost in reason. The red-winged blackbird visited him each time that he was there. In a way, Adam thought of the blackbird as his mother's spirit because it had warned him before there was danger. Adam wondered about Maria every day and knew that he would someday find himself back on the island, looking to meet her again and ask her the many questions that circled about in his mind. The only remnants of the truth laid within Adam's camera. When he felt himself losing a grip on reality and wondering if all had been a very bad dream, he would force himself to look back at those pictures and would remember.

It was the island that had taken his mother, after all. The only way of seeing her again would be to go there, but that is the exact reason why his father had continued going there. It seemed that even being away from the island still trapped his mind in a prison of wonder as his dad always told him. The questions that would never be answered left him feeling empty and going to that place during low tide in hopes that the path would emerge once again.

Acknowledgements

Thank you to the photographer of Charles Island that walked up to me and requested I write this book. Your stories have inspired me to continue writing and sharing the spiritual and paranormal past and present of the island.

I am grateful for the Maryland Writing Association for providing countless workshops and networking opportunities to learn more about publishing and writing.

Finally, thank you to my family and friends for supporting me on my writing journey and always cheering me on and providing feedback. I couldn't do it without you!

Charles Island Disclosure

Charles Island is located in Milford, Connecticut and is a state park. The sandbar (tombolo) between Silver Sands State Park and Charles Island over washes twice daily with tidal flooding which produces dangerous currents and undertow. No one should walk on any portion of the tombolo when it is covered with water.

Attention Hikers!

It is important to know walking all the way to Charles Island is not always possible. Low tides do not always uncover the tombolo completely. See Milford Harbor/Connecticut tide chart for tide details.

NO CROSSING May 1st to September 9th due to natural area preserve for nesting birds!

Turn the page for a sneak peek of how it all began in the 1600's in another Tale of Charles Island:

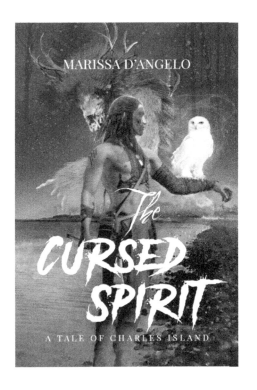

The Cursed Spirit

Catori

1

The brisk emptiness of winter enveloped the land in a white silence. Breaths exhaled formed smoky ghosts within the dry air. Most living had ventured south long before although some braved the harsh season. Each lone branch on the trees reached up for any sliver of warmth they could receive from the sun. They stood tall, but bare.

The Natives respected this land of theirs. For after the dreaded winter would come many fruits to feast on. It was a climate that took years and years of adjustment. Animals were their sole reason for survival as they used their furs for warmth and

nutrients for food. Catori lay beneath some of the

furs and poked his head out.

"Ka'," short for mom in their tribal language.

"Where is dad?" Mom paced around, carrying dried

salmon that had been stored previously. Her long,

dark hair hung down just past her waist and swayed

as she walked around.

"Hunting for deer," she said. He squeezed his

eyes shut as hard as he could, frustrated with himself

for not waking up in time. He was supposed to learn

the ways of his father so he could take care of their

village. After all, he was next in line as chief of their

tribe. Catori was the only child that the chief had

which made everyone extra careful about sending

him out with the others. This only upset him more because it made him feel like a child although he had been alive for seventeen winters.

He decided to go anyway despite how warm the bed was, he jumped out of it and peered underneath to grab day clothes. There was a light brown tunic rested on top of the pile. His mother had made it from a hunt that father went on last year. As he placed it over his head, he could feel someone's eyes on him. Mom was right in front of him with her hands on her hips.

"And what do you think you're doing?" She asked. He got up anyway and started towards the door.

"I'm going to go help Pa," she took the tunic off the shelf before he could get it.

"You don't know where he is. Take the pole, Catori. Maybe there will be some fish." She stepped in front of him and touched his forehead gently.

"I know you want to make your father proud. And you do. Every day. He'll be happy enough with some fish."

He sighed, but agreed. Mom still thought of him as a toddler at times. She pushed the tunic over his head and kissed him on the cheek before sending him off to fish.

Outside was painfully beautiful. The snow from yesterday softened nature's grounds. He took regretful footsteps, ruining the soft surface. With each step, he felt the snow pack down beneath him. It was slightly warmer today so the trees let off the heavy snow that had been weighing their branches down. A nearby stream that led into the ocean was a few trees away. Unlike any other season, there was a dead silence. On a nice spring day, you could hear the birds chirp and fly out from their nests in the full trees. There were still some, but the only sound made were his steps.

When the stream appeared ahead, it was narrow which meant most of its waters were back in the ocean at low tide. The great spirit caused low and high tides. When they were low in the summer, many shells would wash ashore and that meant the spirits were pleased with his tribe. However, when the tides were high, it would take all of those gifts away - teaching his tribe strength and persistence.

In the winter, it was a different story. Higher tides allowed Catori to not have to travel as far in order to fish. Catori came at the wrong time. He continued on anyway as he promised his mom a fish so if he had to, he would venture out further towards the shore.

As he reached the coast, rocks poked out of the snow. They created a path that led to a smaller island. The low tide had revealed a path that he could follow, which was almost too perfect. He paused for a moment and looked out as he said a prayer privately to himself.

Sacred Land, Poquahaug, you have been with my ancestors for many, many winters. The food and land you give us is sacred. We give back each day as a

thank you.

Catori was named after his father saw a spirit of their ancestors from this land. The spirit had warned him not to travel across the pathway since high tide was coming. His life had been saved by that spirit. When his father returned, his mother broke the news of her pregnancy and they were quick to name him spirit in their tribal language: Catori.

Available Now!

About the Author

Marissa is the author of a memoir and the Tales of Charles Island series. Marissa mostly writes fictional stories and began by journaling and writing screenplays in elementary school for her peers to perform. She spends much of her time with her pets aside from traveling to new places and journaling.

Born and raised in Connecticut, she holds New England close to her heart and many of her stories are based in the suburbs of Connecticut.

She has a deep and profound respect for people with special needs as her first job in her field was a special educator. Marissa found her voice through writing. While in high school, she was the editor of the Arts and Entertainment section of the school newspaper. She pursued a degree in Education, minoring in English literature and Anthropology. Later, she went back to school to better understand Autism and graduated with a Master's in Special Education.

Marissa would love to hear from you. Use the links below to connect & hear about upcoming books:

Visit Marissa's Website:
https://www.mystywrites.com/

Instagram:
https://www.instagram.com/_mysty_writes/

Amazon Page:
https://www.amazon.com/author/marissadangelo

Made in the USA
Middletown, DE
18 May 2022